this book belongs to

MY HAPPINESS SCALE

The best part about today
_____
_____
_____
_____
_____
_____
_____

A picture of my day:

I am grateful for....

I am thankful for people, I am thankful for

MY HAPPINESS SCALE

The best part about today

_____

_____

_____

_____

_____

_____

A picture of my day:

I am grateful for....

I am thankful for people

MY HAPPINESS SCALE

The best part about today
_____
_____
_____
_____
_____
_____
_____

A picture of my day:

I am grateful for....

I am thankful for people I

MY HAPPINESS SCALE

The best part about today

A picture of my day:

MY HAPPINESS SCALE

The best part about today
_____
_____
_____
_____
_____
_____
_____
_____

A picture of my day:

I am grateful for....

I am thankful for

people

MY HAPPINESS SCALE

The best part about today
_____
_____
_____
_____
_____
_____
_____

A picture of my day:

I am grateful for....

I am thankful for

people I am thankful for

MY HAPPINESS SCALE

The best part about today _____
_____
_____
_____
_____
_____
_____

A picture of my day:

MY HAPPINESS SCALE

The best part about today
_____
_____
_____
_____
_____
_____
_____

A picture of my day:

I am grateful for....

I am thankful for

people

MY HAPPINESS SCALE

The best part about today
_____
_____
_____
_____
_____
_____
_____

A picture of my day:

MY HAPPINESS SCALE

The best part about today
_____
_____
_____
_____
_____
_____
_____

A picture of my day:

I am grateful for....

I am thankful for

people I am thankful for

MY HAPPINESS SCALE

The best part about today
_____
_____
_____
_____
_____
_____
_____
_____

A picture of my day:

MY HAPPINESS SCALE

The best part about today

A picture of my day:

I am grateful for....

I am thankful for

people I am thankful for

MY HAPPINESS SCALE

The best part about today
_____
_____
_____
_____
_____
_____
_____
_____

A picture of my day:

I am grateful for....

people I am thankful for

MY HAPPINESS SCALE

The best part about today

A picture of my day:

MY HAPPINESS SCALE

The best part about today

A picture of my day:

I am grateful for....

I am thankful for people

MY HAPPINESS SCALE

The best part about today
_____
_____
_____
_____
_____
_____
_____

A picture of my day:

MY HAPPINESS SCALE

The best part about today

A picture of my day:

MY HAPPINESS SCALE

The best part about today

A picture of my day:

MY HAPPINESS SCALE

The best part about today

A picture of my day:

MY HAPPINESS SCALE

The best part about today

A picture of my day:

I am grateful for....

people I am thankful for

MY HAPPINESS SCALE

The best part about today _____
_____
_____
_____
_____
_____
_____
_____

A picture of my day:

I am grateful for....

I am thankful for people I am thankful for

MY HAPPINESS SCALE

The best part about today _____
_____
_____
_____
_____
_____
_____
_____

A picture of my day:

I am grateful for....

I am thankful for

people I am thankful for

MY HAPPINESS SCALE

The best part about today
_____
_____
_____
_____
_____
_____
_____

A picture of my day:

I am grateful for....

people I am thankful for

MY HAPPINESS SCALE

The best part about today
_____
_____
_____
_____
_____
_____
_____

A picture of my day:

MY HAPPINESS SCALE

The best part about today
_____
_____
_____
_____
_____
_____
_____

A picture of my day:

I am grateful for....

I am thankful for

people I am thankful for

MY HAPPINESS SCALE

The best part about today
_____
_____
_____
_____
_____
_____
_____

A picture of my day:

MY HAPPINESS SCALE

The best part about today

A picture of my day:

MY HAPPINESS SCALE

The best part about today
_____
_____
_____
_____
_____
_____
_____
_____

A picture of my day:

I am grateful for....

I am thankful for

people I am thankful for

MY HAPPINESS SCALE

The best part about today

I am grateful for....

I am thankful for

people I am thankful for

MY HAPPINESS SCALE

The best part about today

A picture of my day:

MY HAPPINESS SCALE

The best part about today
_____
_____
_____
_____
_____
_____
_____

A picture of my day:

MY HAPPINESS SCALE

The best part about today
_____
_____
_____
_____
_____
_____
_____

A picture of my day:

MY HAPPINESS SCALE

The best part about today
_____
_____
_____
_____
_____
_____
_____

A picture of my day:

MY HAPPINESS SCALE

The best part about today
_____
_____
_____
_____
_____
_____
_____

A picture of my day:

I am grateful for....

I am thankful for

people I am thankful for

MY HAPPINESS SCALE

The best part about today _____
_____
_____
_____
_____
_____
_____

A picture of my day:

I am grateful for....

I am thankful for

people I am thankful for

MY HAPPINESS SCALE

The best part about today

A picture of my day:

I am grateful for....

I am thankful for

people I am thankful for

MY HAPPINESS SCALE

The best part about today

A picture of my day:

MY HAPPINESS SCALE

The best part about today

A picture of my day:

MY HAPPINESS SCALE

The best part about today
_____
_____
_____
_____
_____
_____
_____

A picture of my day:

I am grateful for....

I am thankful for people

MY HAPPINESS SCALE

The best part about today
_____
_____
_____
_____
_____
_____
_____

A picture of my day:

I am grateful for....

I am thankful for

people I am thankful for

MY HAPPINESS SCALE

The best part about today
_____
_____
_____
_____
_____
_____
_____
_____

A picture of my day:

MY HAPPINESS SCALE

The best part about today

A picture of my day:

MY HAPPINESS SCALE

The best part about today
_____
_____
_____
_____
_____
_____
_____

A picture of my day:

I am grateful for....

I am thankful for people

I am thankful for

MY HAPPINESS SCALE

The best part about today

A picture of my day:

I am grateful for....

I am thankful for

people I am thankful

MY HAPPINESS SCALE

The best part about today
_____
_____
_____
_____
_____
_____
_____

A picture of my day:

I am grateful for....

I am thankful for

people I am thankful for

MY HAPPINESS SCALE

The best part about today
_____
_____
_____
_____
_____
_____
_____
_____

A picture of my day:

MY HAPPINESS SCALE

The best part about today
_____
_____
_____
_____
_____
_____
_____

A picture of my day:

I am grateful for....

I am thankful for people

MY HAPPINESS SCALE

The best part about today
_____
_____
_____
_____
_____
_____
_____

A picture of my day:

I am grateful for....

I am thankful for

people I am thankful for

MY HAPPINESS SCALE

The best part about today
_____
_____
_____
_____
_____
_____
_____
_____

A picture of my day:

I am grateful for....

I am thankful for people

MY HAPPINESS SCALE

The best part about today

A picture of my day:

I am grateful for....

I am thankful for

people I am thankful for

MY HAPPINESS SCALE

The best part about today

A picture of my day:

I am grateful for....

I am thankful for

people I am thankful for

MY HAPPINESS SCALE

The best part about today
_____
_____
_____
_____
_____
_____
_____

A picture of my day:

MY HAPPINESS SCALE

The best part about today

A picture of my day:

MY HAPPINESS SCALE

The best part about today

A picture of my day:

MY HAPPINESS SCALE

The best part about today
_____
_____
_____
_____
_____
_____
_____

A picture of my day:

I am grateful for....

I am thankful for people

MY HAPPINESS SCALE

The best part about today _____
_____
_____
_____
_____
_____
_____

A picture of my day:

I am grateful for....

people I am thankful for

MY HAPPINESS SCALE

The best part about today _____
_____
_____
_____
_____
_____
_____
_____

A picture of my day:

I am grateful for....

people I am thankful for

MY HAPPINESS SCALE

The best part about today

A picture of my day:

I am grateful for....

people I am thankful for

MY HAPPINESS SCALE

The best part about today

A picture of my day:

I am grateful for....

I am thankful for

people I am thankful for

MY HAPPINESS SCALE

The best part about today
_____
_____
_____
_____
_____
_____
_____

A picture of my day:

I am grateful for....

I am thankful for people

MY HAPPINESS SCALE

The best part about today
_____
_____
_____
_____
_____
_____
_____

A picture of my day:

MY HAPPINESS SCALE

The best part about today

A picture of my day:

I am grateful for....

I am thankful for

people I am thankful for

MY HAPPINESS SCALE

The best part about today

A picture of my day:

I am grateful for....

I am thankful for people

MY HAPPINESS SCALE

The best part about today _____

_____

_____

_____

_____

_____

_____

_____

A picture of my day:

I am grateful for....

people I am thankful for

MY HAPPINESS SCALE

The best part about today

A picture of my day:

MY HAPPINESS SCALE

The best part about today

_____

_____

_____

_____

_____

_____

_____

A picture of my day:

MY HAPPINESS SCALE

The best part about today _____
_____
_____
_____
_____
_____
_____
_____

A picture of my day:

MY HAPPINESS SCALE

The best part about today
_____
_____
_____
_____
_____
_____
_____

A picture of my day:

I am grateful for....

people I am thankful for

MY HAPPINESS SCALE

The best part about today

A picture of my day:

MY HAPPINESS SCALE

The best part about today _____
_____
_____
_____
_____
_____
_____

A picture of my day:

MY HAPPINESS SCALE

The best part about today

A picture of my day:

I am grateful for....

I am thankful for people I

MY HAPPINESS SCALE

The best part about today
_____
_____
_____
_____
_____
_____
_____

A picture of my day:

I am grateful for....

I am thankful for
people

MY HAPPINESS SCALE

The best part about today
_____
_____
_____
_____
_____
_____
_____

A picture of my day:

I am grateful for....

I am thankful for

people I am thankful for

MY HAPPINESS SCALE

The best part about today

A picture of my day:

Made in the USA
Middletown, DE
22 December 2017